Lindbergh
and the Spirit of St. Louis

Bruce LaFontaine

DOVER PUBLICATIONS, INC.
Mineola, New York

Published in Canada by General Publishing Company, Ltd., 30 Lesmill Road, Don Mills, Toronto, Ontario.
Published in the United Kingdom by Constable and Company, Ltd., 3 The Lanchesters, 162–164 Fulham Palace Road, London W6 9ER.

Bibliographical Note

Lindbergh and the Spirit of St. Louis is a new work, first published by Dover Publications, Inc., in 1999.

International Standard Book Number: 0-486-40567-2

Manufactured in the United States of America
Dover Publications, Inc., 31 East 2nd Street, Mineola, N.Y. 11501

INTRODUCTION

On May 20-21, 1927, a 25-year-old airmail pilot and Air Corps Reserve officer named Charles Lindbergh literally flew into the history books. His nonstop solo flight across the Atlantic Ocean, from New York to Paris, may seem tame by today's standards, but at the time his achievement electrified people throughout the world. "Slim" Lindbergh's solitary journey over thousands of miles of open ocean was an unprecedented technical achievement and a tribute to the young man's courage and skill.

Lindbergh's airplane, which he named the *Spirit of St. Louis,* was specially designed and built by the Ryan Aircraft Corporation for the transatlantic journey. The *Spirit* had to be flown with little or no direct forward vision because the entire front end of the aircraft was taken up by immense fuel tanks. Lindbergh relied solely on side windows and a small periscope for navigation. The flight was demanding and exhausting. The young pilot kept himself awake for more than 33 hours, from Roosevelt Field on Long Island, New York, to Le Bourget Airport outside Paris. Even in those early days before television had created a "global village," Lindy's achievement made him an instant worldwide celebrity. Before the flight some in the press had labeled Lindbergh the "Flyin' Fool"; now he was the Lone Eagle. Thousands of prizes, awards, medals, accolades, and gifts of all kinds were given to him by everyone from King George VI of Great Britain to the mayor of Little Falls, Minnesota (his hometown). The Army Air Corps promoted him to the rank of colonel in the Reserves.

After his historic flight, Charles Lindbergh went on to make a number of significant contributions to the development of aviation. With Anne Morrow Lindbergh, his wife and lifelong flying partner, he went on long-distance exploration and survey missions for Pan American Airways. The Lindberghs charted new air routes from the United States to South America, Europe, and across the Pacific Ocean to Asia. Lindy also helped Pan Am develop its fleet of flying boats, the famous China Clipper and other amphibious aircraft used to fly from continent to continent. The avalanche of publicity that came with the kidnapping and murder of the Lindberghs' baby in 1932, eventually forcing them to seek refuge in England. The family lived abroad from 1936 until 1939.

Anne Morrow Lindbergh was a remarkable woman in her own right. Though she was a generally silent partner in her husband's aeronautical ventures she developed for herself a writing career that has spanned more than 60 years. Her first book was *North to the Orient,* an evocative account of the couple's flight from New York to Tokyo via the northern circle, published in 1935. Since then dozens of her books have been published, including the best-selling *Gift from the Sea* (1954), an essay on the challenges and opportunities facing modern women. Among Anne Morrow Lindbergh's other books are collections of her poems and letters, writings from her diary, memoirs, essays, meditations, and fiction. Like her husband, she was beloved by millions of Americans.

To his own and his wife's later regret, Charles Lindbergh became enmeshed in U.S. politics in the late 1930s. He echoed the beliefs of his father, a congressman (1907–1917) who opposed American entry into World War I, by forcefully advocating U.S. neutrality in the growing conflict between Germany and the Allies. At the same time he was ahead of his time in advocating the strengthening of U.S. air power. Reacting to President Franklin D. Roosevelt's criticism of him and the isolationist America First Committee, which he supported, Lindbergh resigned his Air Corps commission. It was during this period that many Americans accused him of being not only pro-Nazi but also, based on statements he had made, anti-Semitic. His unwillingness to mount a public defense against these charges dogged him for the rest of his life.

After Japan and Germany declared war on the U.S. in December 1941, Lindbergh declared his wholehearted support of the country's war effort. Denied a return to military service because of his prewar activities, he became an adviser to aircraft manufacturers, first Ford Motor Company and then United Aircraft Corporation. For the latter company he helped in the development of the famed F-4U Corsair fighter, which he flew in combat against the Japanese. Even though he was still a civilian, he also flew combat missions in the P-38 Lightning fighter for the Army Air Corps. Based on these experiences, he devised ways to get the most efficient use out of fuel so that the planes could stay airborne for longer periods of time. His wartime service won praise from all quarters, and President Dwight Eisenhower appointed him a brigadier general in the Air Force Reserve in 1954. Just a year before, Lindbergh's book about his great flight, *The Spirit of St. Louis,* had been published. This exciting, occasionally mystical memoir won a Pulitzer Prize.

Ever the pioneer, Lindbergh was one of the first airmen to recognize the importance of rocketry. From 1929 on, he lent his support to Robert Goddard's experiments with unmanned flight, and after World War II his was a strong voice among those urging increased research into rockets and missiles. At the same time his concern for the environment led him to oppose further U.S. development of the supersonic transport (SST) passenger airplane. "I would rather have birds than airplanes," he once wrote. Charles Lindbergh remained an active participant in the aviation industry until his death on August 26, 1974, at age 72.

Charles Augustus Lindbergh, Jr. was born in Detroit, Michigan, on February 4, 1902. His parents were Evangeline Lodge Land, a schoolteacher, and Charles Augustus Lindbergh, a lawyer who was soon to become a United States Congressman (1907–1917). Charles spent much of his boyhood on the family farm in Little Falls, Minnesota. There he developed a love of the outdoors and of machines, especially airplanes. Young Charles is shown at age six with his mother and at age eight with his father.

In 1920 Charles entered the University of Wisconsin at Madison, where he showed a keen in interest in mechanics and motorcycles. But after only two years he left college to pursue his true passion, airplanes. He took flying lessons in Nebraska under the instruction of J.H. Lynch, shown above with the 20-year-old "Slim"—a nickname Lindbergh had acquired owing to his slender frame and 6-foot-3-inch height. After attaining his pilot's license, Lindbergh became partners with Lynch in the stunt-flying business. Here the "barnstormers" are shown in front of their aircraft, a Lincoln-Standard Tourabout biplane.

Lindbergh toured the Midwest during 1922–1923 with another young aviator pal, Bud Gurney. Together they put on stunt flying exhibitions and made parachute jumps. They also performed dangerous aerial acrobatics, including "wing-walking" (shown above) and hanging upside down from the landing gear struts. The most popular stunt flying aircraft of this era was the reliable and manueverable Curtiss JN-4 "Jenny," shown above. During this period Lindbergh's barnstorming provided just enough money for him to eat and buy fuel, but he was learning valuable flying skills that would serve him well in his later career.

In 1924 Lindbergh joined the United States Army Air Service to gain further experience in more advanced military aircraft. He took his flight training at Brooks Air Field, Texas, where he was commissioned a second lieutenant. While flying an SE-5 fighter plane, shown above, Lindy collided with another aircraft during a mock dogfight. Both pilots parachuted to safety.

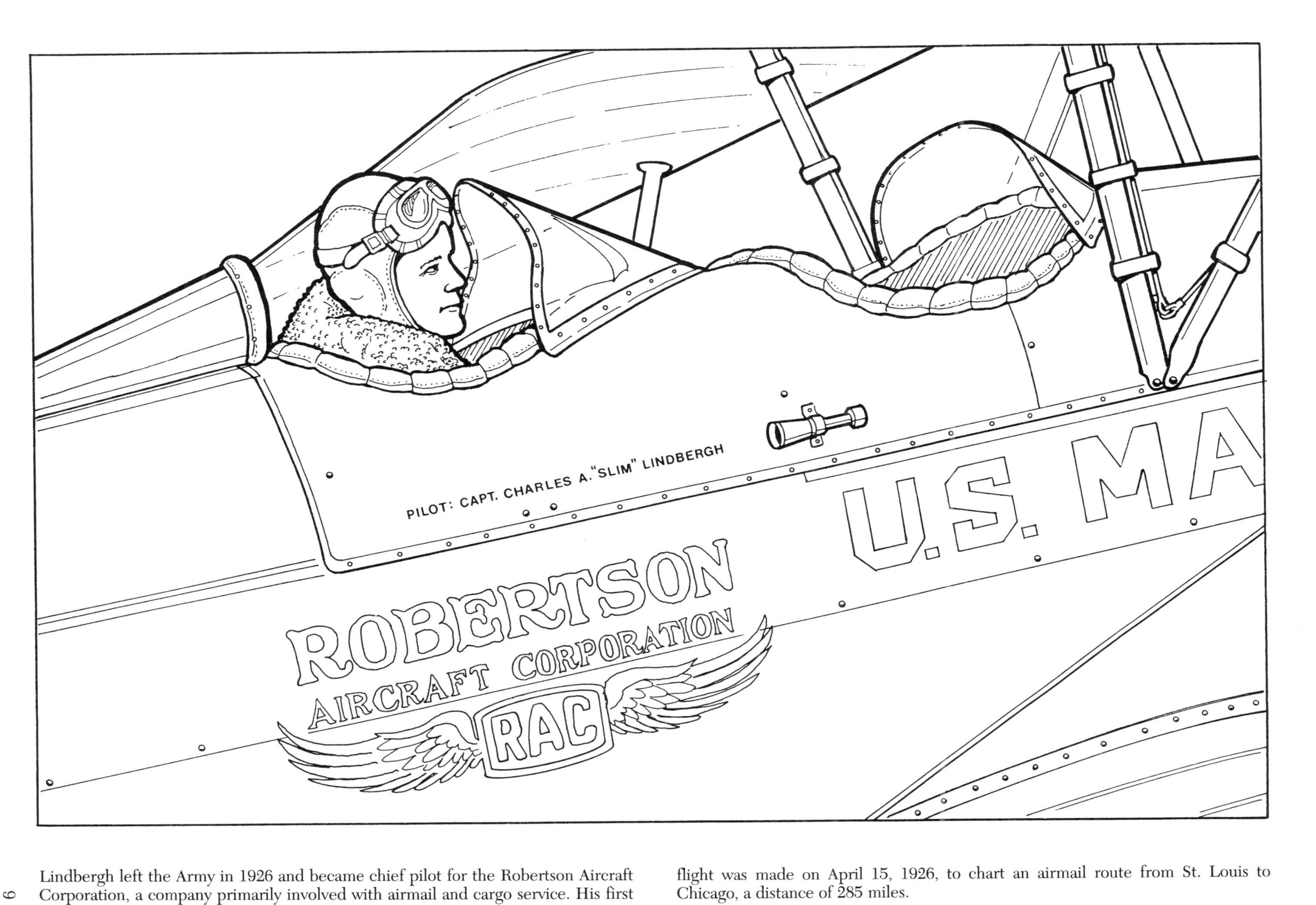

Lindbergh left the Army in 1926 and became chief pilot for the Robertson Aircraft Corporation, a company primarily involved with airmail and cargo service. His first flight was made on April 15, 1926, to chart an airmail route from St. Louis to Chicago, a distance of 285 miles.

Airmail pilots knew they were in a dangerous business. The World War I surplus aircraft they flew, such as the De Havilland DH-4 shown above, were old and increasingly unreliable. During this risky era, 31 out of the first 40 airmail pilots died while flying these old aircraft. Lindbergh survived several crash landings and bailouts while flying the mail route. Soon he became known as "Lucky Lindy."

In 1919 a wealthy New York hotel owner of French ancestry, Raymond Orteig, offered a prize of $25,000 to the first aviator to fly nonstop across the Atlantic Ocean from New York to Paris. This became the incentive for many aircraft companies and pilots to attempt the long-distance flight. Charles Lindbergh won financial backing from a group of businessmen in St. Louis and then worked with the Ryan Aircraft Company in developing an airplane to make the flight. The historic craft they built was the Ryan NYP, christened the *Spirit of St. Louis* by Lindbergh.

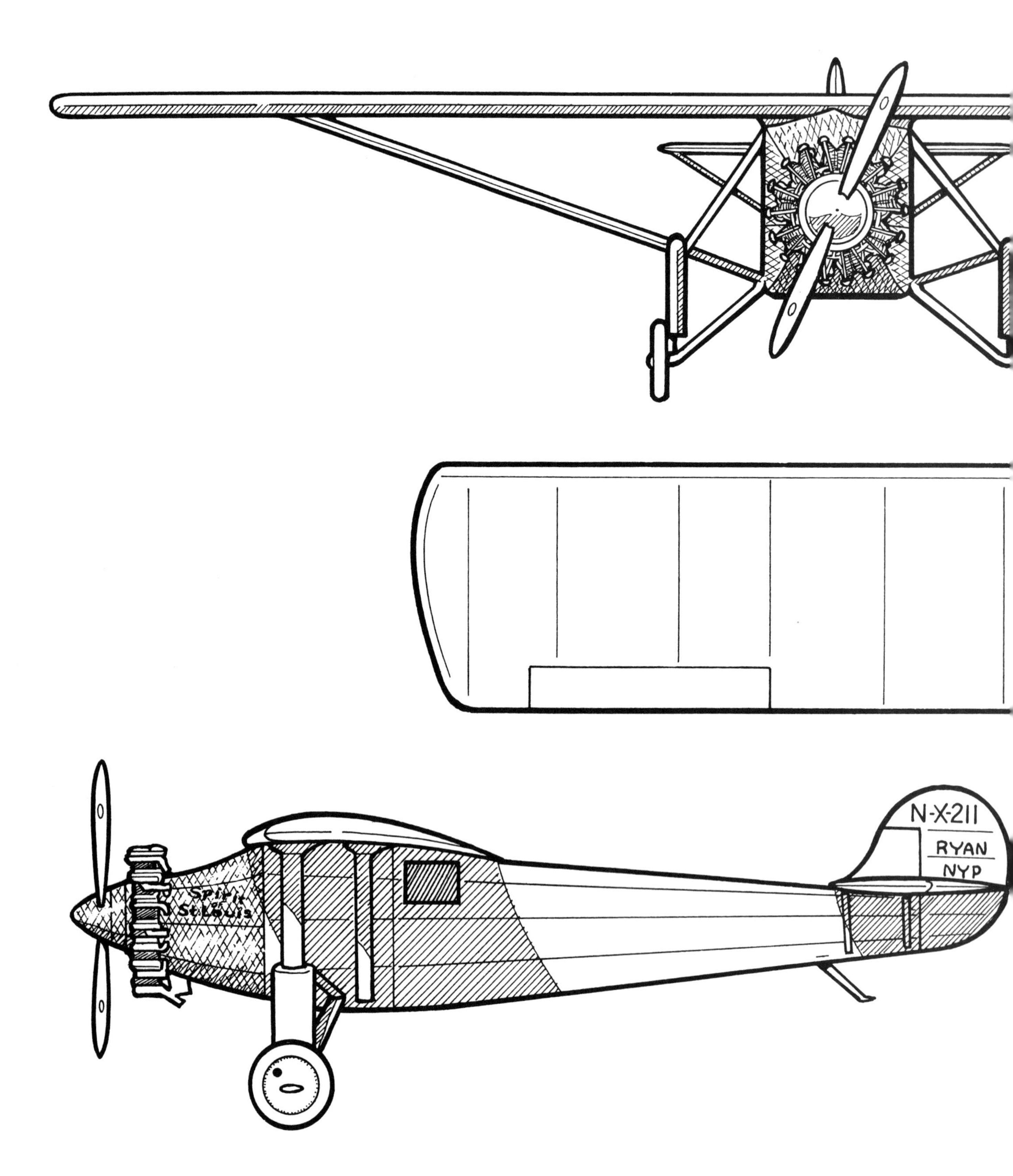

The *Spirit of St. Louis* was a high-winged monoplane powered by a Wright J-5 "Whirlwind" nine-cylinder radial engine. The engine developed 223 horsepower and gave the *Spirit* a top speed of 129 miles per hour. The internal structure of the fuselage was built of welded steel tubes, covered with fabric and then coated with a special paint, "airplane dope." The skin of the forward fuselage (the cowling) was constructed of aluminum burnished by a rotating steel brush into the distinctive pattern shown. The wing structural ribs were made from spruce and covered with the same coated fabric as the fuselage. The wingspan was 46 feet, and the fuselage was 27 feet 8 inches in length. The aircraft had one main fuel tank and four auxiliary tanks holding a total of 450 gallons.

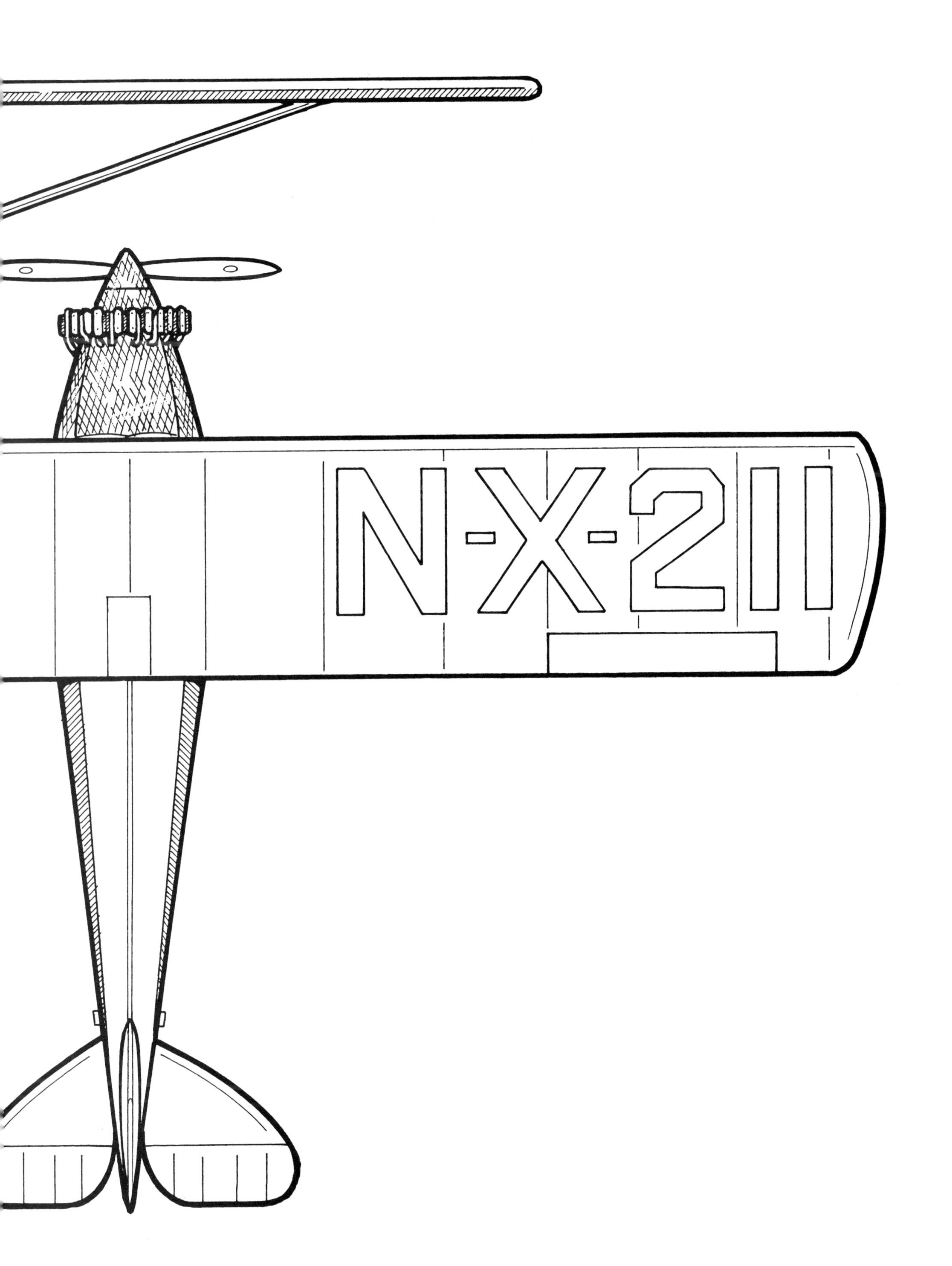
N-X-211

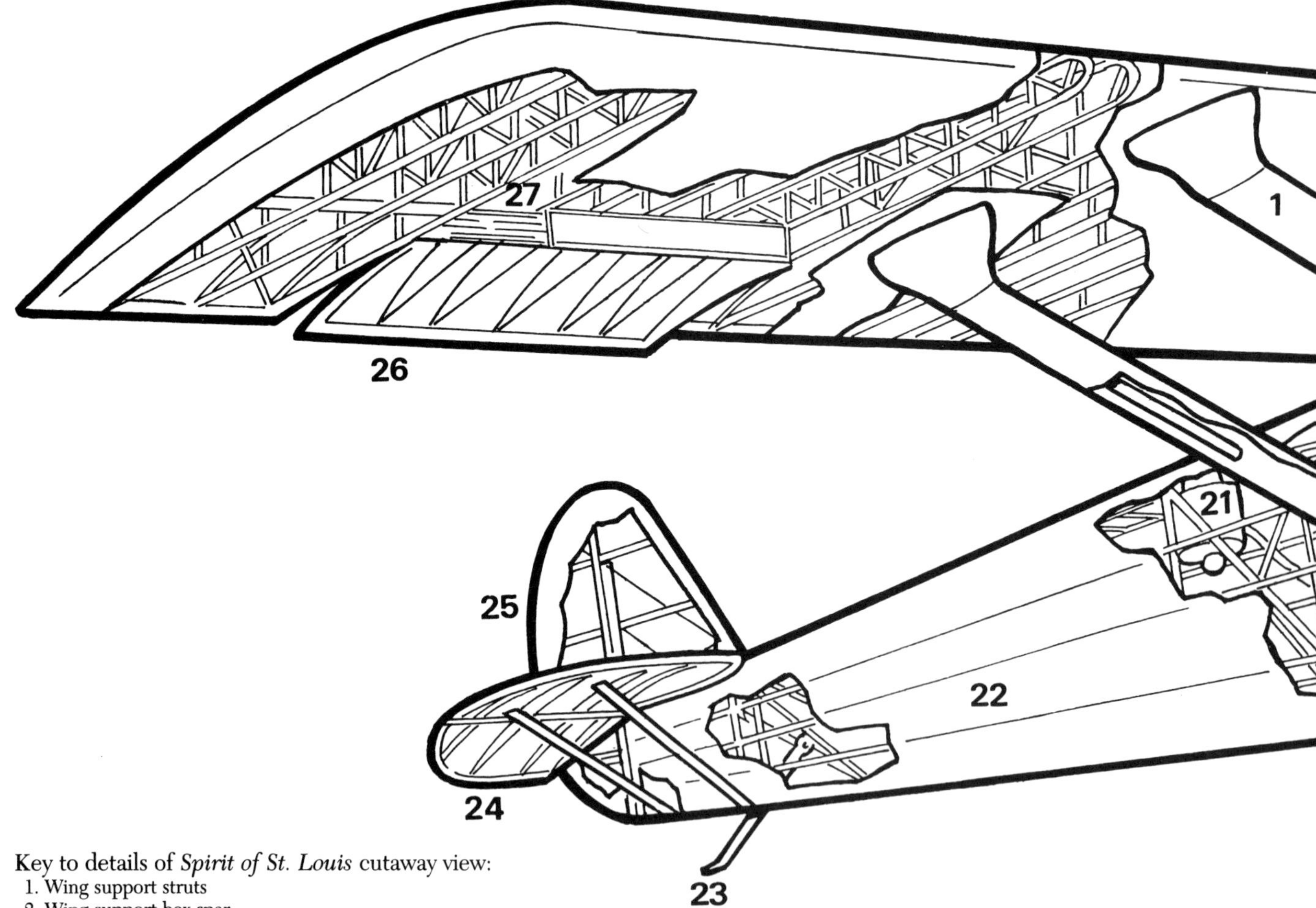

Key to details of *Spirit of St. Louis* cutaway view:
1. Wing support struts
2. Wing support box spar
3. Wing-mounted fuel tank
4. Magnetic compass
5. Instrument panel
6. Periscope for forward viewing
7. Main fuel tanks
8. Aluminum forward fuselage cowling
9. Oil tank
10. Wright J-5 "Whirlwind" 9-cylinder, 223-hp engine
11. Duralumin propeller
12. Aluminum propeller spinner cover
13. Carburetor
14. Landing gear support struts
15. Wire wheels with fabric wheel covers
16. Landing gear shock absorbers
17. Rudder control pedal
18. Control stick
19. Wicker pilot seat
20. Welded steel-tube fuselage structure
21. Earth induction compass
22. Fabric fuselage skin coated with "airplane dope" paint
23. Tail skid
24. Elevator
25. Rudder
26. Aileron
27. Wing support ribs

2
3
4
5
6
7
8
7
9
10
11
12
13
14
15
16
17
18
19

The *Spirit* was built at the Ryan plant in San Diego, California, in February and March of 1927. It was based on an earlier successful Ryan aircraft, the M-2 mail plane. After the *Spirit*'s completion and flight-testing, Lindy flew the airplane to St. Louis and then on to New York. In doing so, he established a new transcontinental flight record of 21 hours and 40 minutes. Lindbergh chose Roosevelt Field, on Long Island, as his operational base because it had the long runway he needed to get his heavy (5,000 pounds) plane into the air.

On the morning of May 20, 1927, Lindbergh took off from rain-soaked Roosevelt Field. The *Spirit,* heavily laden with fuel, barely cleared the trees at the end of the runway. His takeoff had ignited worldwide attention, with the public hoping and praying that the intrepid flyer would be successful.

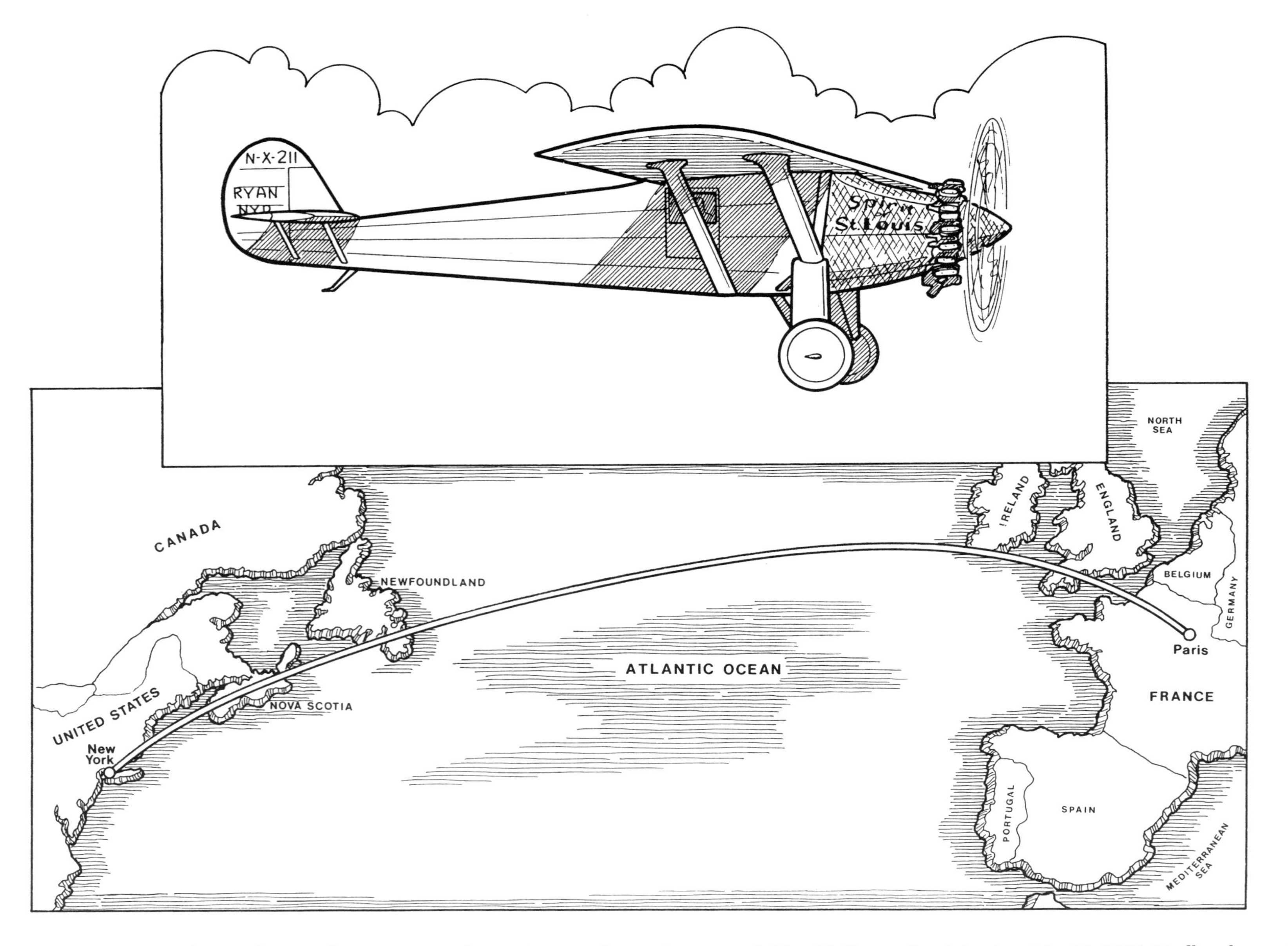

Lindy's flight path took him north over the Canadian provinces of Nova Scotia and Newfoundland, and then out over the open Atlantic. This highly dangerous, solitary flight earned him another nickname, "Lone Eagle." After many hours fighting fatigue, he finally spotted the coast of Ireland. From there, he navigated over England, into France, and then followed the Seine River to Paris. He landed at Le Bourget airfield at 10:22 p.m. (local time) on May 21, 1927. Lindbergh was stunned by the crowd of over 100,000 spectators that lined the airfield. He had covered the transatlantic distance of 3,600 miles in 33 hours and 30 minutes. From that moment on, the courageous young pilot became the most famous and admired man in the world.

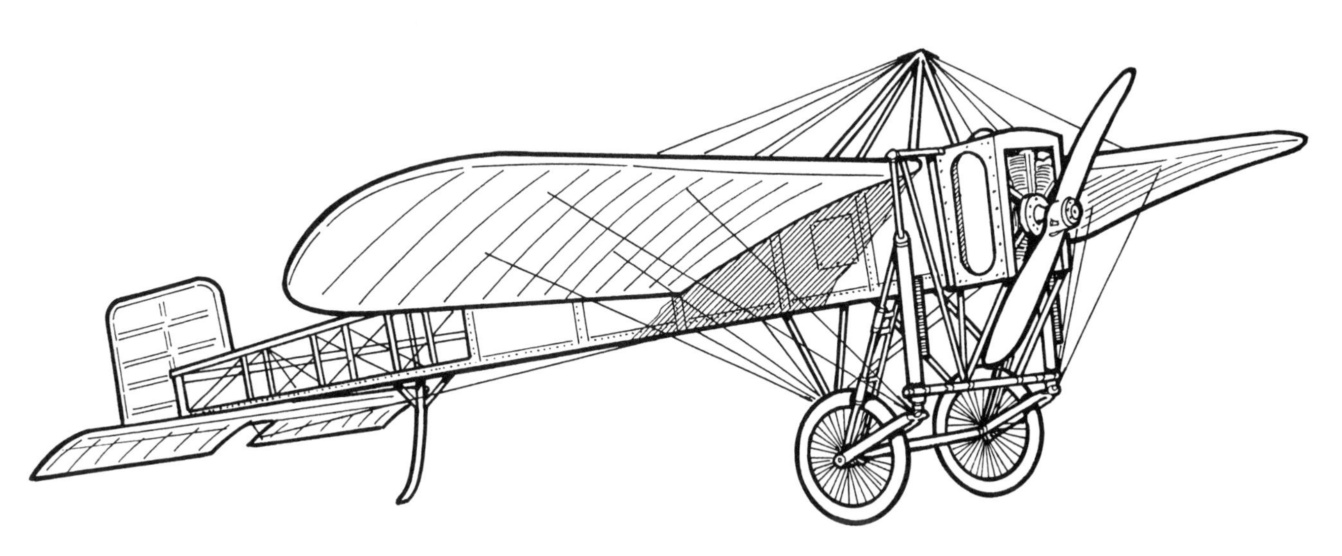

Lindbergh's historic achievement gained him honors and awards throughout Europe and the United States. In France, he was awarded the Legion of Honor. He is shown meeting with another great aviation pioneer, Louis Blériot, the first man to fly across the English Channel. Blériot accomplished his mission in 1909, flying a XI monoplane, shown above.

After visiting England, Lindbergh and the *Spirit* began the return trip to the United States aboard the U.S. Navy cruiser *Memphis.* Lindy and his plane arrived in Washington, D.C., on June 11th. President Calvin Coolidge awarded Lindbergh the Distinguished Flying Cross for his achievement. On June 14, the Lone Eagle was welcomed by New York City with a ticker tape parade attended by over 4 million spectators. A blizzard of paper, 1,800 tons, rained down on the hero from the skyscrapers along Broadway.

On November 14, 1927, Lindbergh became the ninth man in 40 years to receive the Hubbard Medal of the National Geographic Society, here presented by President Calvin Coolidge. Lindy also received a special Gold Medal from the U.S. Congress as well as dozens of other awards, prizes, and medals from nations and cities throughout the world.

Beginning in December of 1927 Lindbergh flew the *Spirit* on a goodwill tour of Central and South America. His first stop was Mexico, where he met Anne Morrow, the daughter of the United States ambassador to Mexico. (She later became his wife and lifelong flying partner.) Lindbergh continued on to visit Guatemala, El Salvador, Honduras, Nicaragua, Costa Rica, and Panama. The *Spirit* is shown above flying over a portion of the Panama Canal. Lindy completed his tour with stops in Colombia, Venezuela, and Cuba.

Close-up view of the engine and cowling of the *Spirit of St. Louis*, displaying flags of all the countries visited by Lindbergh and his historic airplane.

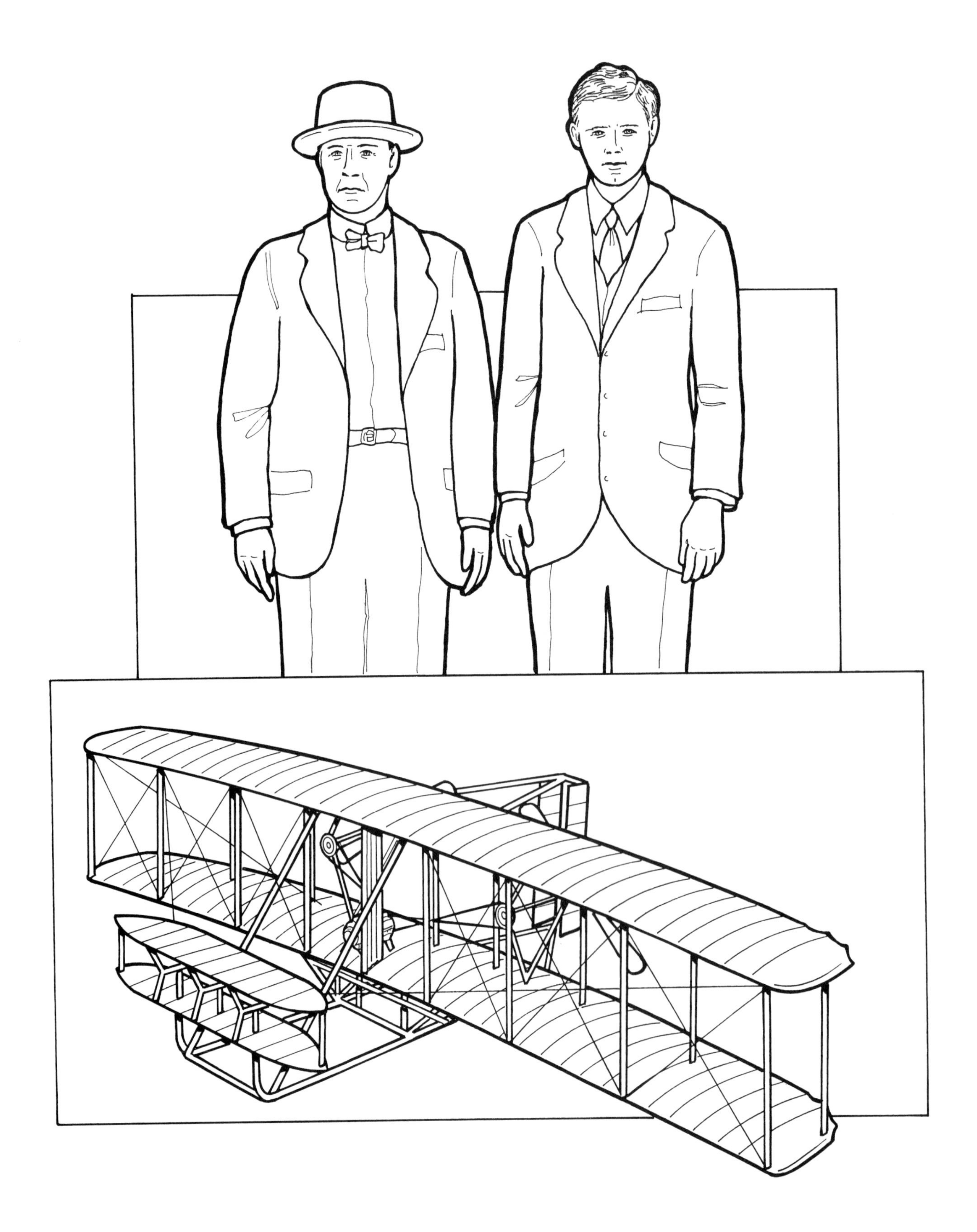

Lindy met with one of the founders of modern aviation, Orville Wright, at the International Civil Aeronautics Conference in Washington, D.C., 1928. Orville and his brother Wilbur revolutionized air transportation with their history-making first powered-airplane flight. They flew a spindly biplane of their own construction, the Wright "Flyer I," pictured above. It flew for just 12 seconds on December 17, 1903. Those brief seconds of flight were the foundation for all subsequent progress in aviation—and later, longer flights by the Wright brothers—including Lindbergh's own record-breaking achievement.

Charles Lindbergh married Anne Morrow in 1929. She became his invaluable partner not only in marriage but also in many aviation activities. In April of 1930, with Anne as his back-seat navigator, Lindy flew the advanced and speedy Lockheed Aircraft Corporation Sirius on a record-breaking 14-hour-and-23-minute flight from California to New York.

Lindy and Anne are shown in their furry, insulated flying suits necessary to ward off the chill of high-altitude flight in open-cockpit aircraft. Their Lockheed Sirius was modified after they made the record-setting transcontinental flight. It was retrofitted with aerodynamic sliding-glass canopies to close off the cabin, making long-distance flights much more comfortable and less tiring.

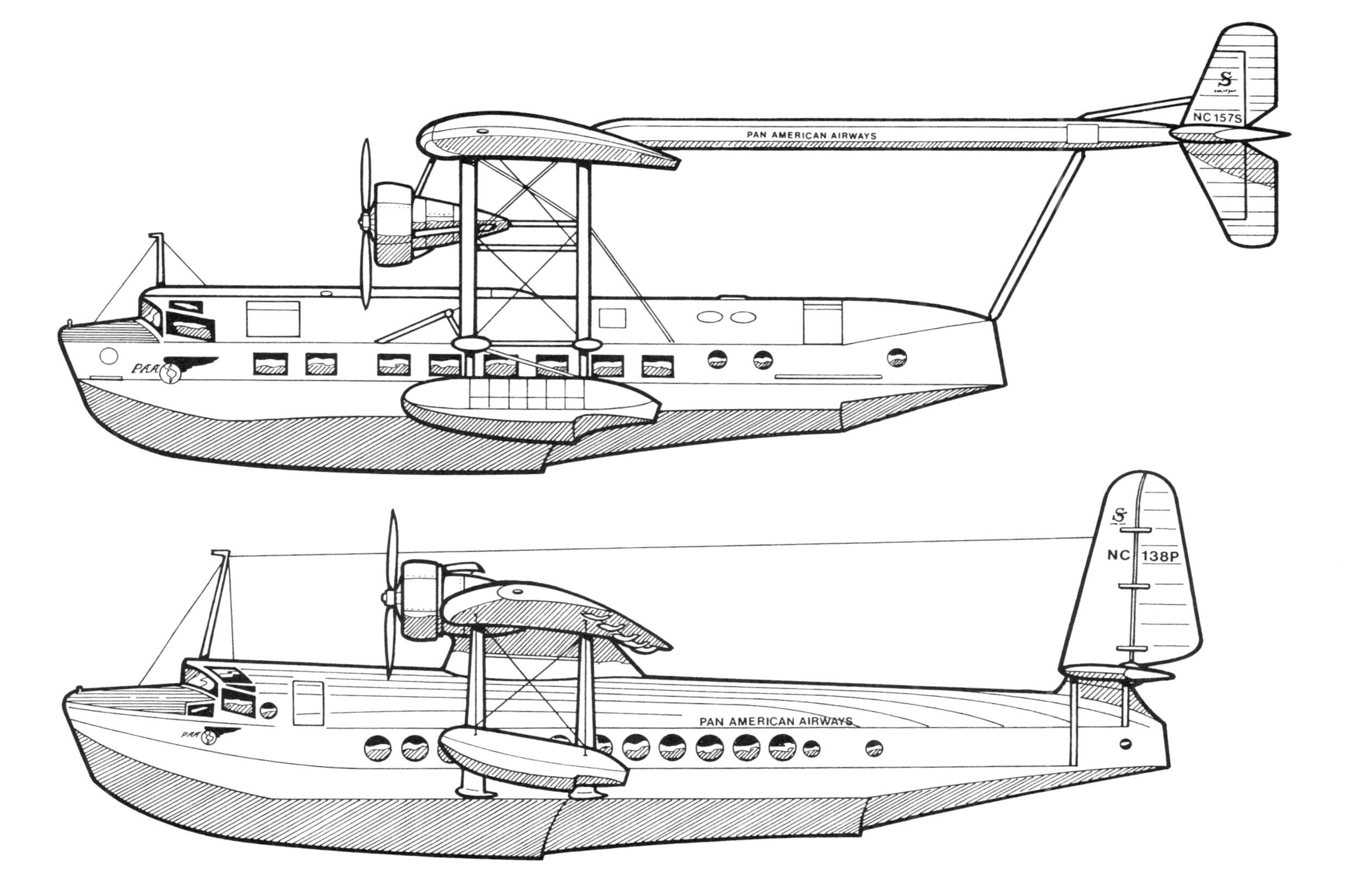

Lindbergh became a technical adviser to Pan American Airways in 1929, and during the early 1930s, he flew a number of aircraft on exploratory missions to Central and South America, charting new air routes for the company. Pan American had developed a large fleet of flying boats. These passenger- and cargo-carrying aircraft had boat-shaped fuselages, or hulls, enabling them to take off and land on water. Pan Am chose flying boats as airliners for two main reasons. First, in case of mechanical breakdown or engine failure (not uncommon in those early days), a flying boat could land on the water. The second reason was the relative scarcity of airports during this era. However, all coastal cities had well-developed harbors and ports that could be utilized by the flying boats as air terminals.

In 1931, Lindbergh flew one of Pan Am's most advanced new flying boats on a South American survey mission. Shown at the top is the Sikorsky S-40. This four-engine airliner could carry 38 passengers over a distance of 900 miles at a cruising speed of 115 mph. Pan American began their long history of naming airliners "clippers" with the S-40 American Clipper. Shown below the S-40 is its successor, the Sikorsky S-42. This flying boat could carry 32 passengers a distance of 1,200 miles at a speed of 150 mph. The Brazilian Clipper was an S-42. The airline later went on to utilize larger and faster flying boats, including the famous Martin M-130 China Clipper and the enormous Boeing 314 Yankee Clipper, both flown over the Pacific Ocean to Asia.

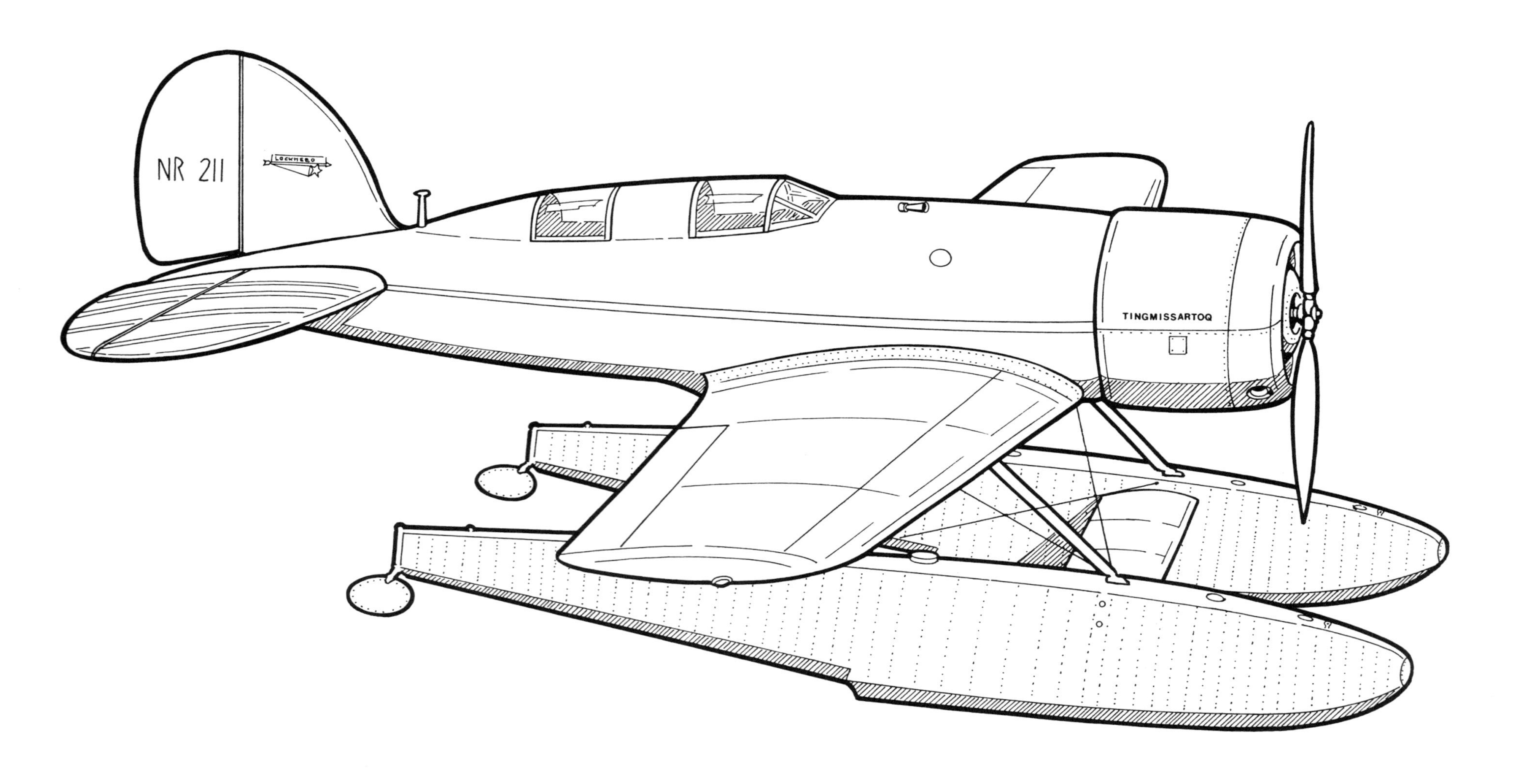

Beginning in 1931, Charles and Anne Lindbergh undertook the first of two major exploration flights for Pan American Airways. Their first journey was made to survey a northern circle route to Asia. In order to facilitate flying and landing over uncharted territory, their Lockheed Sirius had its aerodynamically "spatted" landing wheels removed and replaced with large pontoon floats for water landing. Their flight began on July 27, 1931, and took them from New York to Maine, across Canada to Alaska, then over the Bering Sea to the Kamchatka Peninsula, in the Soviet Union. The couple then journeyed down the Kuril Islands chain, finally arriving in Tokyo on August 26.

The Lindberghs' next record-breaking flight was designed to chart a northern circle route to Europe. As she had done before, Anne Morrow Lindbergh acted as copilot and navigator. On July 9, 1933, she and Charles departed from Long Island, New York. Their route took them to Labrador, Greenland, Iceland, and finally to Copenhagen, Denmark. During their stop in Labrador the Sirius was nicknamed by an Eskimo boy *Tingmissartoq*, meaning "one who flies like a big bird." The Lindberghs liked the name and had it painted on the side of the aircraft.

After reaching Europe, Charles and Anne stopped in Paris and returned home by way of Portugal, the Azores Islands, Gambia (West Africa), and finally across the South Atlantic to Brazil. They then flew up South and Central America to the United States. They finally reached Pan American's seaplane base in Miami on December 16, 1933. Their demanding survey flight had covered an incredible 30,000 miles.

Tingmissartoq moored at Holsteinborg, Greenland, in July 1933.

During the years just before World War II, Charles Lindbergh had taken a strong public stance for American neutrality. After the United States entered the war in December 1941, Lindbergh announced his staunch support of the American war effort. Unfortunately, because of his prewar statements, the War Department refused to reactivate his Army Air Force commission as a pilot. Nevertheless, Lindy was determined to be part of the fight. He became a technical adviser for the United Aircraft Company, working in the Pacific Theater of Operations, testing and developing their hot new Navy fighter, the F-4U Corsair. The Lone Eagle flew this fast and manueverable fighter on a number of Navy combat missions. He then became an instructor and adviser to the U.S. Army Air Force, flying the Lockheed P-38 "Lightning" (shown above). Despite his civilian status and age (42), Lindy flew over 50 combat missions in the P-38, shooting down a number of Japanese aircraft. For the remainder of his lifetime, Lindbergh continued to act as a technical consultant for the military. He was involved in the development of numerous advanced jet aircraft and missiles and in promoting the advancement of aviation.

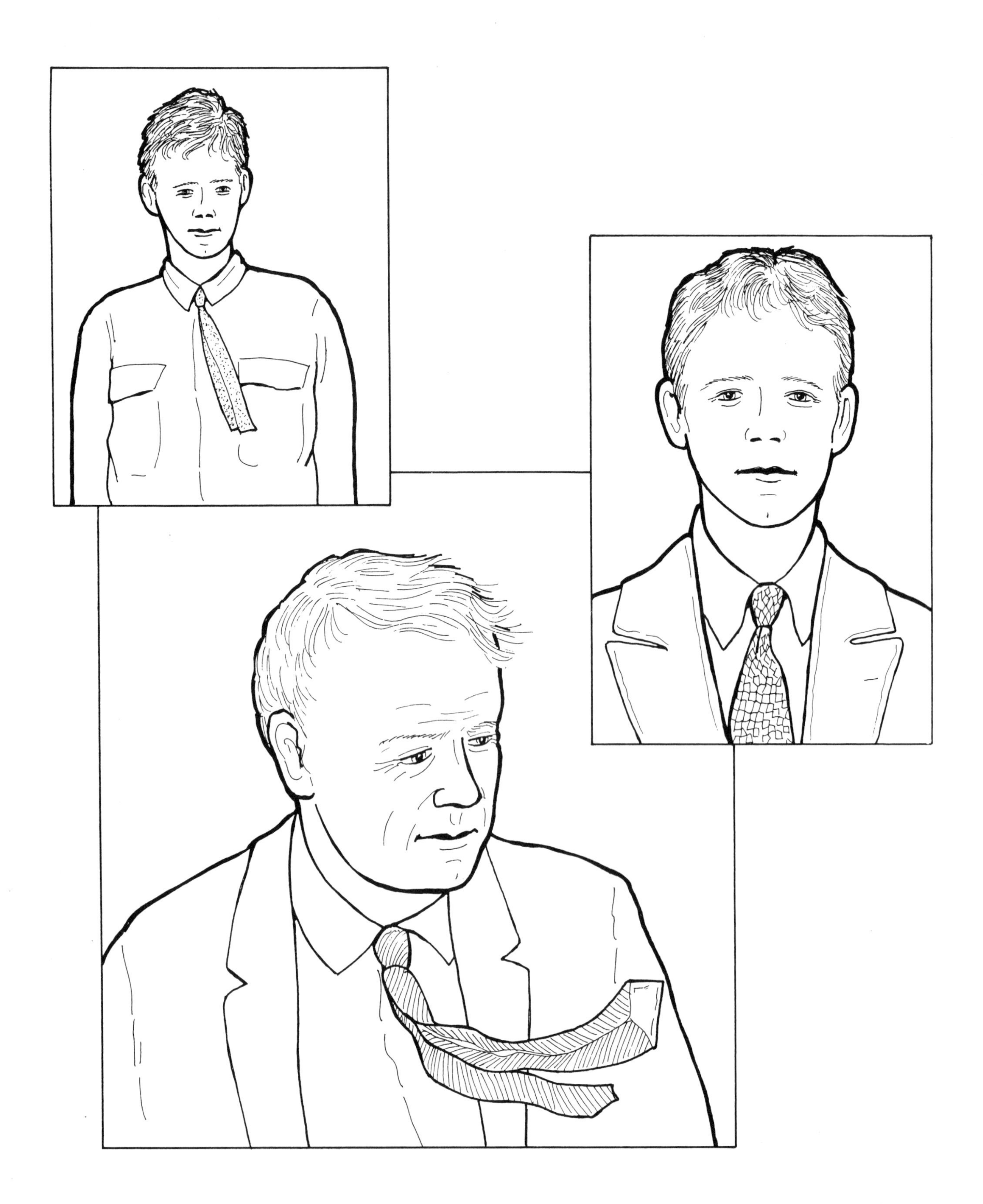

Charles Augustus Lindbergh, Jr. passed away on August 20, 1974, at the age of 72. He died at his home on the Hawaiian Island of Maui with his beloved Anne by his side. The Lone Eagle of the Air is shown above at age 20, age 30, and age 72. He will always be remembered as a true American hero.